How Giraffe became so Tall

Adapted from an original East African folklore tale

D0795533

Retold by Andrea Florens

Illustrated by Claire Norden

Long, long ago in Africa, the Giraffe was much the same size as
the other antelope that wandered the veld.
Except for his tawny-orange patches, he looked quite like a zebra,
or a kudu. And like them, he ate the grass and
plants he could find on the ground.

Now one year,
the **African sun** was
particularly fierce and
not one drop of rain
fell from the sky.

The earth became dry,
and the plants and grass
shrivelled in the heat.
The animals grew very
hungry and had to
squabble over the food
that they could find.

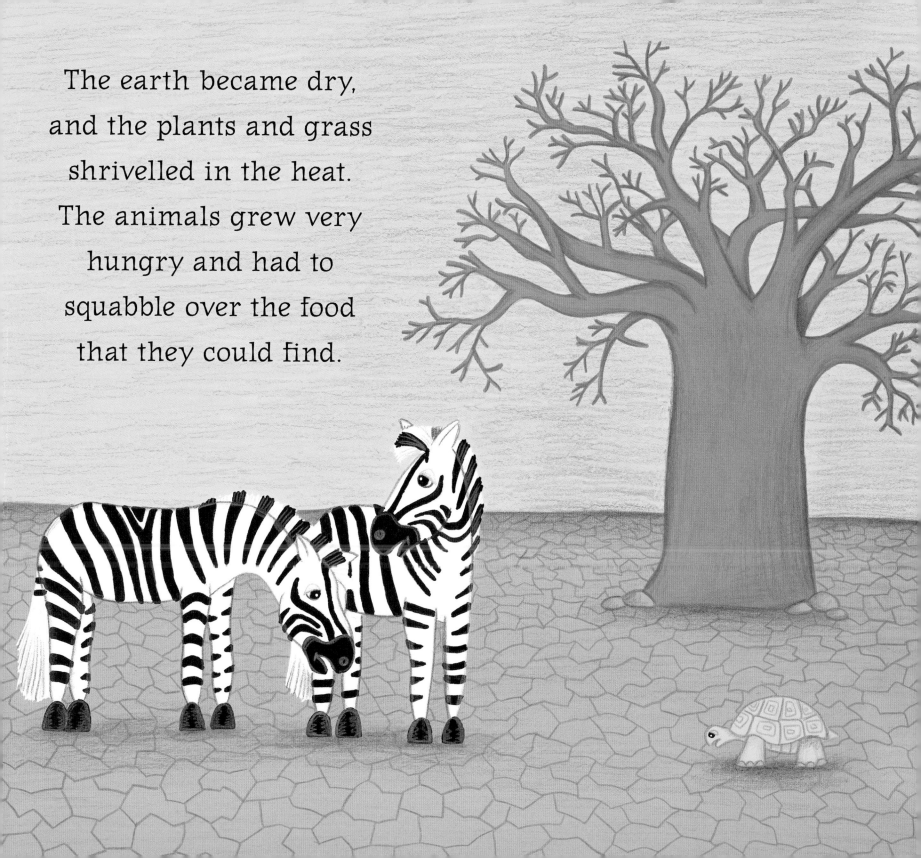

One day, Giraffe was searching for food with his **best friend** the Rhinoceros. Here and there, they found a dry tuft of grass to **nibble** on, or a bush of crunchy leaves to **munch** on.

And being such good friends, they always **shared** what they could find.

"Hurumph!" moaned Rhino chewing on a very dry twig. "Soon there will be no food left."

"You're right," sighed Giraffe "If only we could reach the top of those acacia trees. There are plenty of green leaves up there!"

"I've got an idea!" blurted Rhino proudly, "Let's visit the Magic Medicine Man in the village. He'll help us reach those juicy green leaves, I'm sure of it!"

crunch crunch

"What a brilliant idea my old friend!" praised Giraffe,
and off they set immediately towards the setting sun and in the
direction of the Magic Medicine Man's village.

Trudging along
the dusty trail, the two
friends noticed a grasshopper
leaping from rock to rock.

"Do you see how high he leaps?" whispered Giraffe, "If we could
leap so high, we would reach the top of the acacia trees with
no trouble at all!" Rhino snorted with laughter,
"Indeed we could, but what a funny sight we
would be!" Giraffe laughed too and on they went.

Not long after, they came across a troop of monkeys, swinging high in the tree tops with the help of their long tails. "Mmmm" pondered Rhino, "Now if we had tails like those monkeys, swinging to the top of the acacia trees would be no trouble at all!"

This time Giraffe roared with laughter at the thought, and soon the two friends were on their way again, giggling as they walked. Into the night they travelled, the full moon lighting the long path to the village of the Magic Medicine Man.

Further along the way, a big night owl swooped in front of them before landing high on the bough of a tree. Giraffe and Rhino looked at each other, "Wings!" they said simultaneously, and then they both collapsed with raucous laughter at the thought.

As dawn broke the African sky, the two animals reached the hut of the Magic Medicine Man. He listened to their story, and after a moment's thought, he told the animals to return to him at midday.

Hungry after the long journey, the two friends decided to go in different directions in search of food, promising to call the other if they found some.

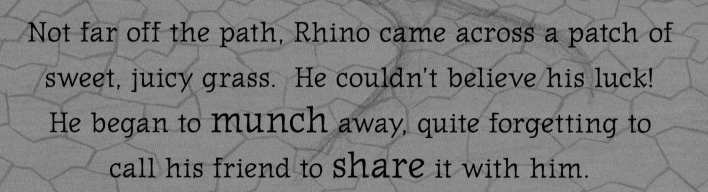

Not far off the path, Rhino came across a patch of sweet, juicy grass. He couldn't believe his luck! He began to munch away, quite forgetting to call his friend to share it with him.

munch
munch

Giraffe was not so lucky to find food, and at midday he walked wearily back to the village. There the Magic Medicine Man had prepared a magical mixture of leaves and roots. "Once you've eaten this, you will be able to reach the tallest acacia trees" said the kind Magic Medicine Man. Then he and Giraffe waited for Rhino to arrive.

After a long while, the Magic Medicine Man said, "The magic will not work much longer. Rhino is late. You will have to eat this all by yourself." And so Giraffe began to munch, and as he did, the strangest thing happened. He felt a tingling in his legs ... and a stretching in his neck ...

munch munch

... and as he stood chewing on
the magic mixture ... his legs grew taller and taller ...
and his neck grew longer and longer,
until he stood towering above
the Magic Medicine Man
and his little hut.
"Yahoo!" shouted Giraffe with joy,
"Thank you, thank you!
Now I'll have plenty to eat."

Just then, Rhino came strolling along, his tummy full from all the delicious grass he'd greedily eaten by himself. When he realised there was no more magic mixture for him, he became very angry and chased after

the Magic Medicine Man as far as he could.

To this day, the Giraffes are the tallest animals in the world, able to reach the highest branches for their food. Due to Rhino's jealousy, he is no longer friends with Giraffe. And when Rhino sees Man, he's likely to chase after him as far as he can.

Produced by Art Publishers (Pty) Ltd
Durban, Johannesburg, Cape Town
All rights reserved. No part of this publication may be reproduced in any form without the prior written consent of the publisher.